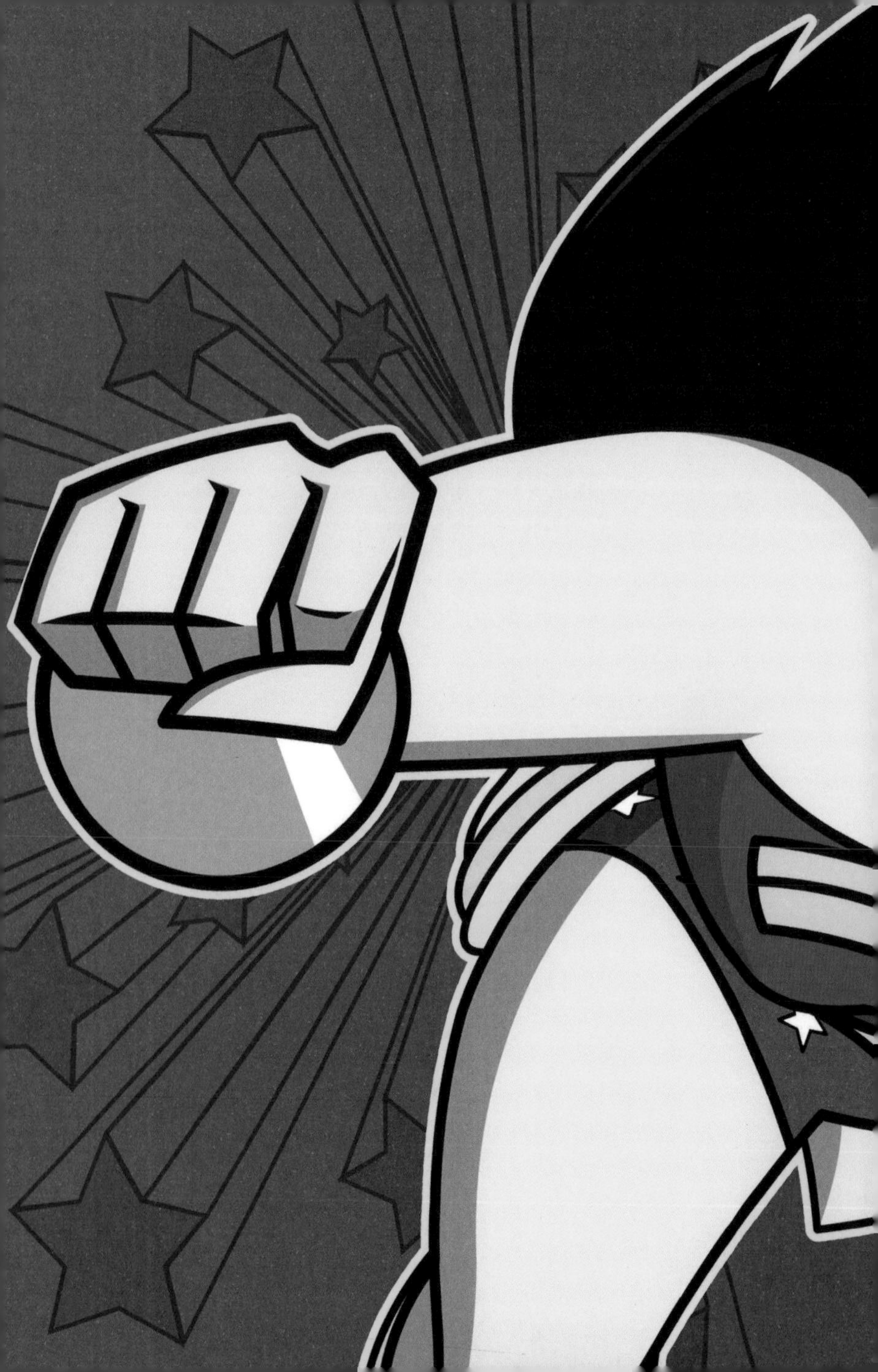

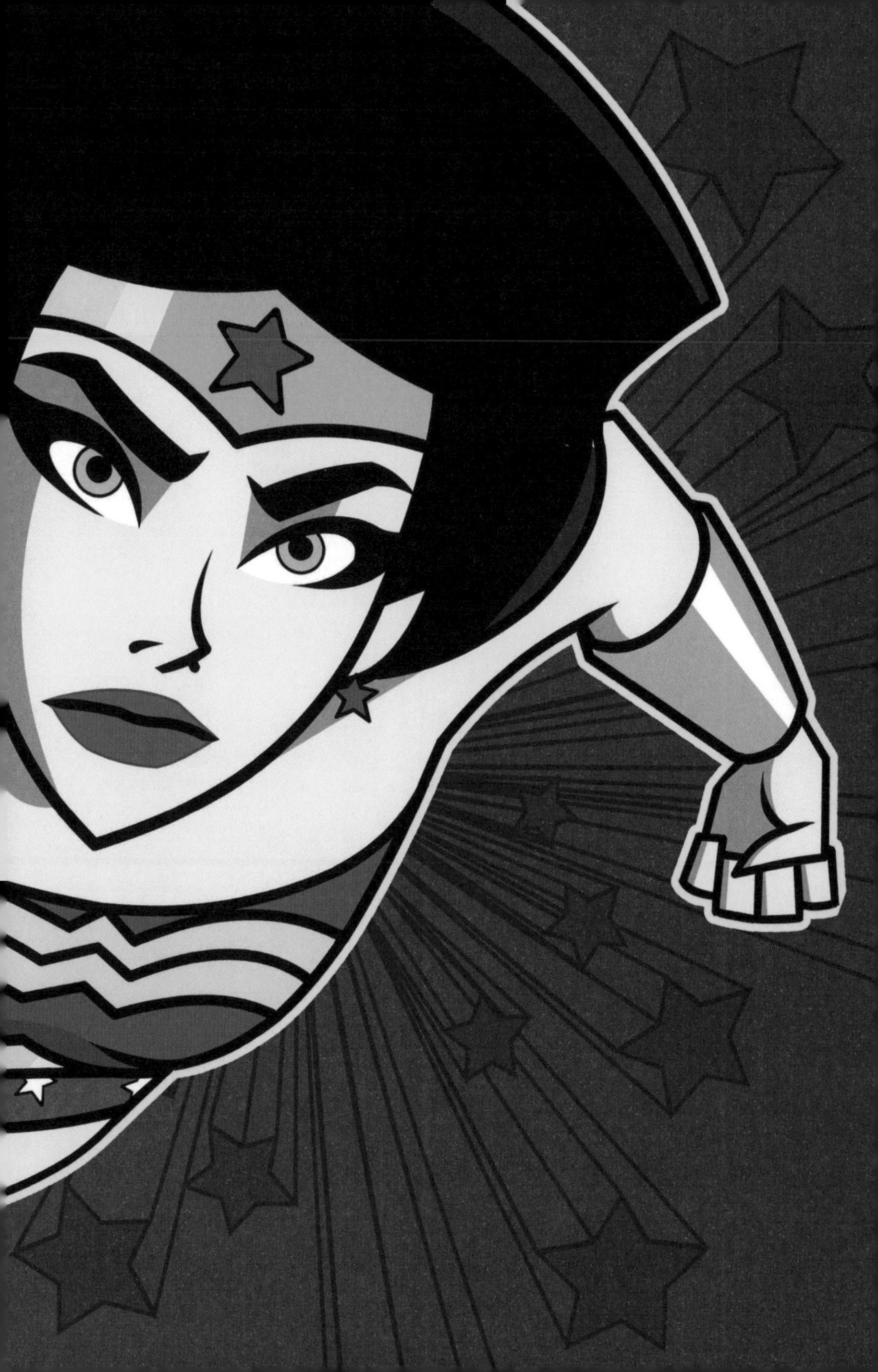

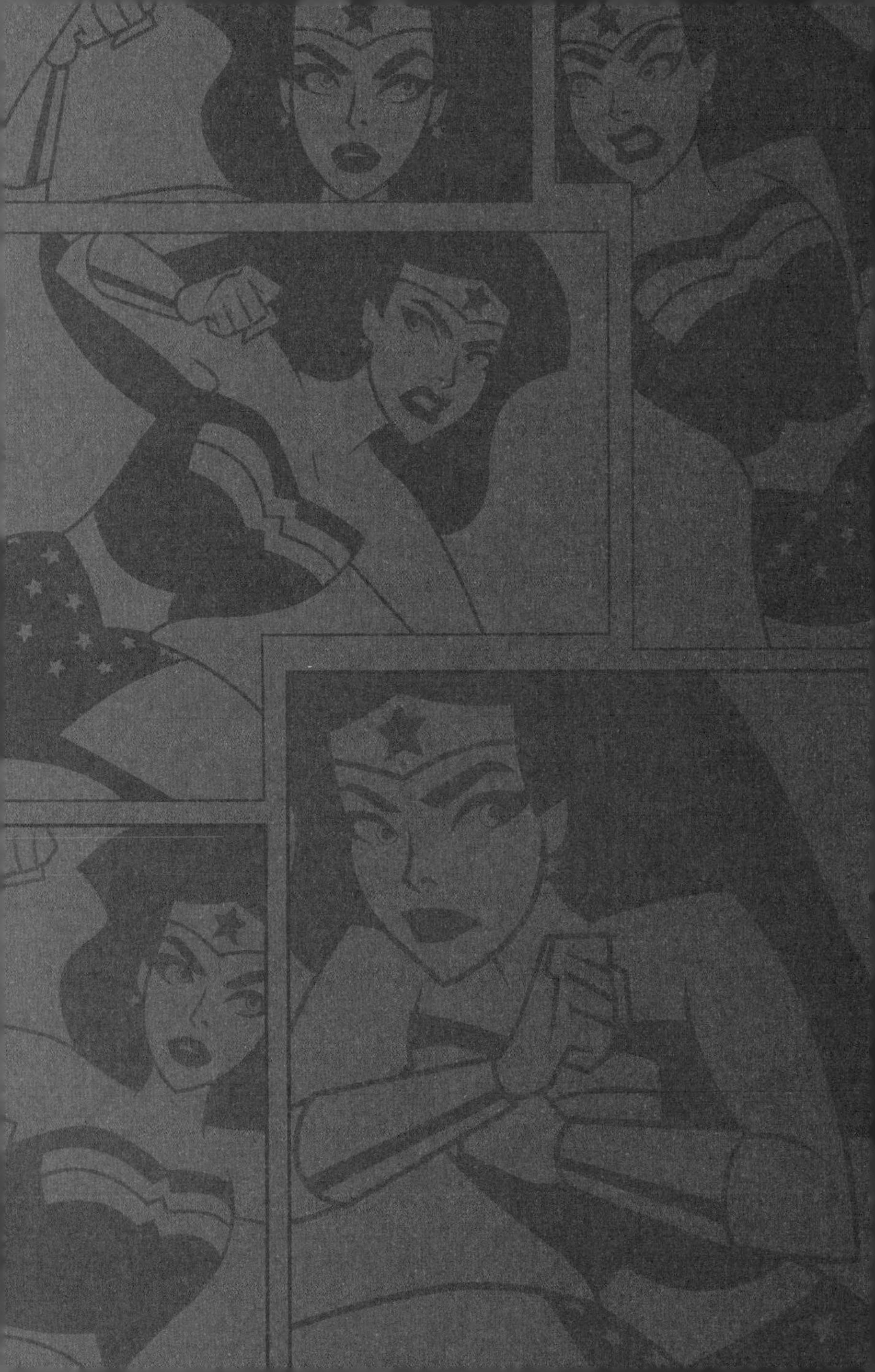

DC SUPER HEROES

WONDER WOMAN™

DR. PSYCHO'S CIRCUS OF CRIME

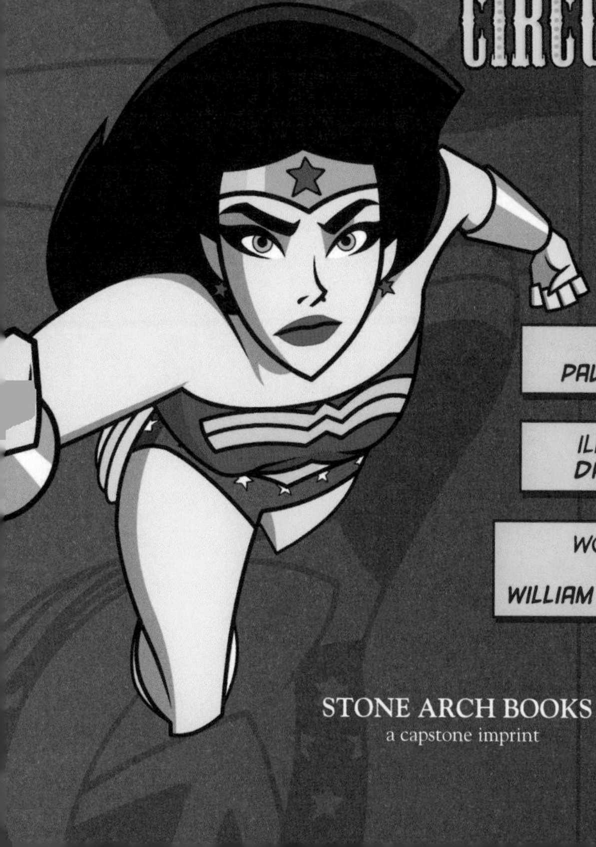

WRITTEN BY
PAUL KUPPERBERG

ILLUSTRATED BY
DAN SCHOENING

WONDER WOMAN
CREATED BY
WILLIAM MOULTON MARSTON

STONE ARCH BOOKS
a capstone imprint

Published by Stone Arch Books
A Capstone Imprint
1710 Roe Crest Drive
North Mankato, Minnesota 56003
www.capstonepub.com

214

Cataloging-in-Publication Data is available on the Library of Congress website.
ISBN: 978-1-4342-2761-4 (paperback)

Summary: When a crime wave erupts in Washington D.C., Wonder Woman investigates and discovers a strange connection between the cases — each criminal had recently visited the circus! The Amazon Princess goes undercover under the big top, and soon learns that the evil Dr. Psycho is brainwashing the audience into committing crimes. If Wonder Woman can't stop him, the Capital City will quickly become a three-ring circus.

Art Director: Bob Lentz
Designer: Kay Fraser

Printed and bound in the USA.
214

TABLE OF CONTENTS

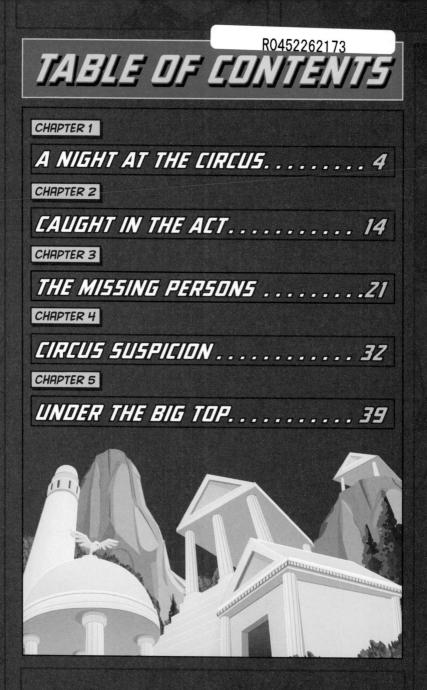

CHAPTER 1

A NIGHT AT THE CIRCUS

"I'm so glad you decided to take the night off and come to the circus!" said Etta Candy to her friend Princess Diana. She and Diana crossed the crowded fairway of the Bartleby Brothers Circus. Lights brightened the night, and the air was filled with music, laughter, and the sweet smell of cotton candy.

"I am too," replied the Amazon Princess. "I've never been to a circus before."

Etta stopped in her tracks and gasped. "Really?" she asked.

"We didn't have circuses where I grew up," said Diana, the super hero also known as Wonder Woman.

"Are you kidding me?" asked Etta.

"Of course not," Diana replied. "When I was a little girl on the island of Themyscira, we made up our own games and staged tournaments with one another."

"That sounds like fun," Etta said. "What kind of games?"

"Oh, waterfall diving, blindfolded races through the forest, and wild bear wrestling," replied Diana with a shrug. "You know, the usual stuff."

Etta stared at her friend and said, "You wrestled . . . bears?"

"Well," Diana began, "not the fully grown ones, but —" **THUD!**

Without warning, a red-haired man wearing a plaid shirt, blue jeans, and a yellow baseball cap bumped into Diana. He hit her hard enough to send her stumbling back a step.

"Excuse me, sir," Diana began, but the man glanced nervously at her and kept walking.

"Hey, pal!" Etta shouted after him. "Don't you have any manners?!"

"Don't be so angry, Etta," Diana said. "He seems nervous. I hope he's all right."

"Humph!" Etta said. "How can you be so nice to someone who's so rude?"

Diana smiled and let out a little laugh. "Perhaps that's why I was chosen to be the Amazon ambassador of peace to the rest of the world," she said.

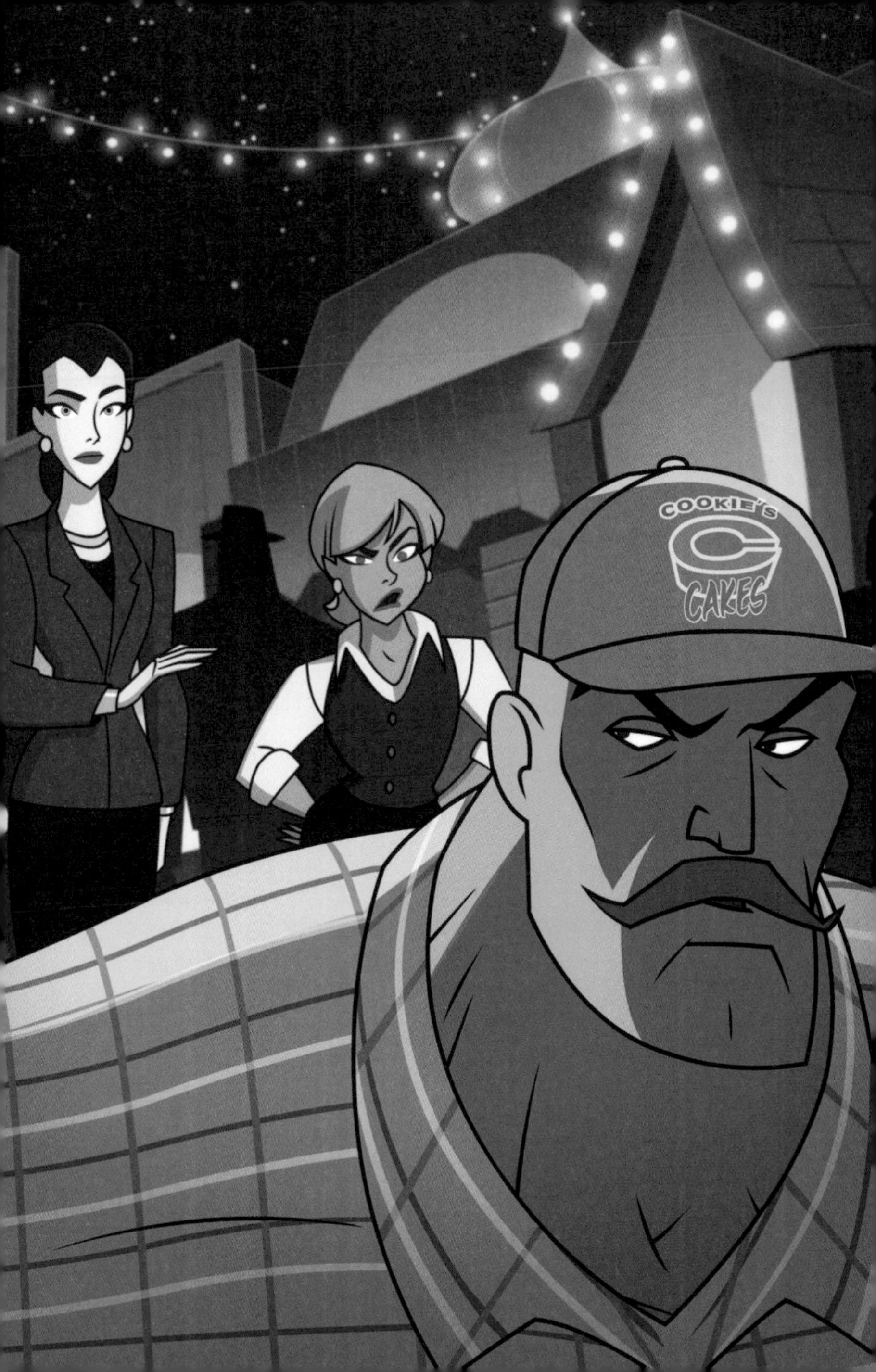
COOKIE'S
CAKES

"But anyone can learn to be kinder and more forgiving," Diana added.

"Okay, okay," Etta said with a grin. "Now let's get inside. The real show is about to begin."

*   *   *

Princess Diana had been born on the island of Themyscira, home to the race of mighty women warriors known as Amazons. As gifts for her birth, the gods of mythology had given the child the beauty of Aphrodite, the wisdom of Athena, the speed of Hermes, and the strength of Hercules. Diana grew to become the bravest, most skilled of all Amazon warriors. However, she never forgot the most important lesson — to only use her warrior powers when peaceful solutions had already failed.

First and foremost, Wonder Woman was a messenger of peace. This fact was in the front of Diana's mind whenever her help was needed.

The day after her circus visit was one of those days. Diana had been called by the police to the Garden Galleria, a large shopping mall. She was dressed in her familiar red, blue, and yellow Wonder Woman uniform. Atop her head was a golden tiara. Around each wrist she wore a silver bracelet, and her Golden Lasso rested on her hip.

"Thanks for coming, Wonder Woman," said Police Lieutenant David Schorr. Schorr had dark hair and wore a black suit. He was shorter than Wonder Woman and his fellow police officers, but he had the confidence of a giant.

"Sorry to bother you with this," the lieutenant said. "We usually only call when it's something too big for the police department to handle."

"What seems to be the problem?" Wonder Woman asked.

"Please follow me," the lieutenant said.

They walked through the entryway of the Galleria. The large, open shopping mall branched off into three levels of stores. The shops had all been locked up the night before, protected by electronically controlled metal gates.

Schorr stopped and pointed. They were now standing in front of Jameson Jewelers. It was like any other store in the Galleria, except for one thing — its gate had been ripped from the wall!

The heavy, metal gates were laying in a twisted heap on the tile floor. "Oh, my!" said Wonder Woman in surprise.

"We think this was done by a human," said Lieutenant Schorr. "A really strong one. We found his handprints in the metal. The person also robbed several other stores nearby. Between these robberies and a bunch of other cases I've got, I'm stumped."

"Surely a security guard heard something or a security camera caught the thieves at work?" Wonder Woman said.

"The mall doesn't have any guards, just an electronic security system that they turn on at night," said Lieutenant Schorr.

"What's this?" Wonder Woman asked.

She pointed to a flash of yellow peeking out from under the wrecked gate.

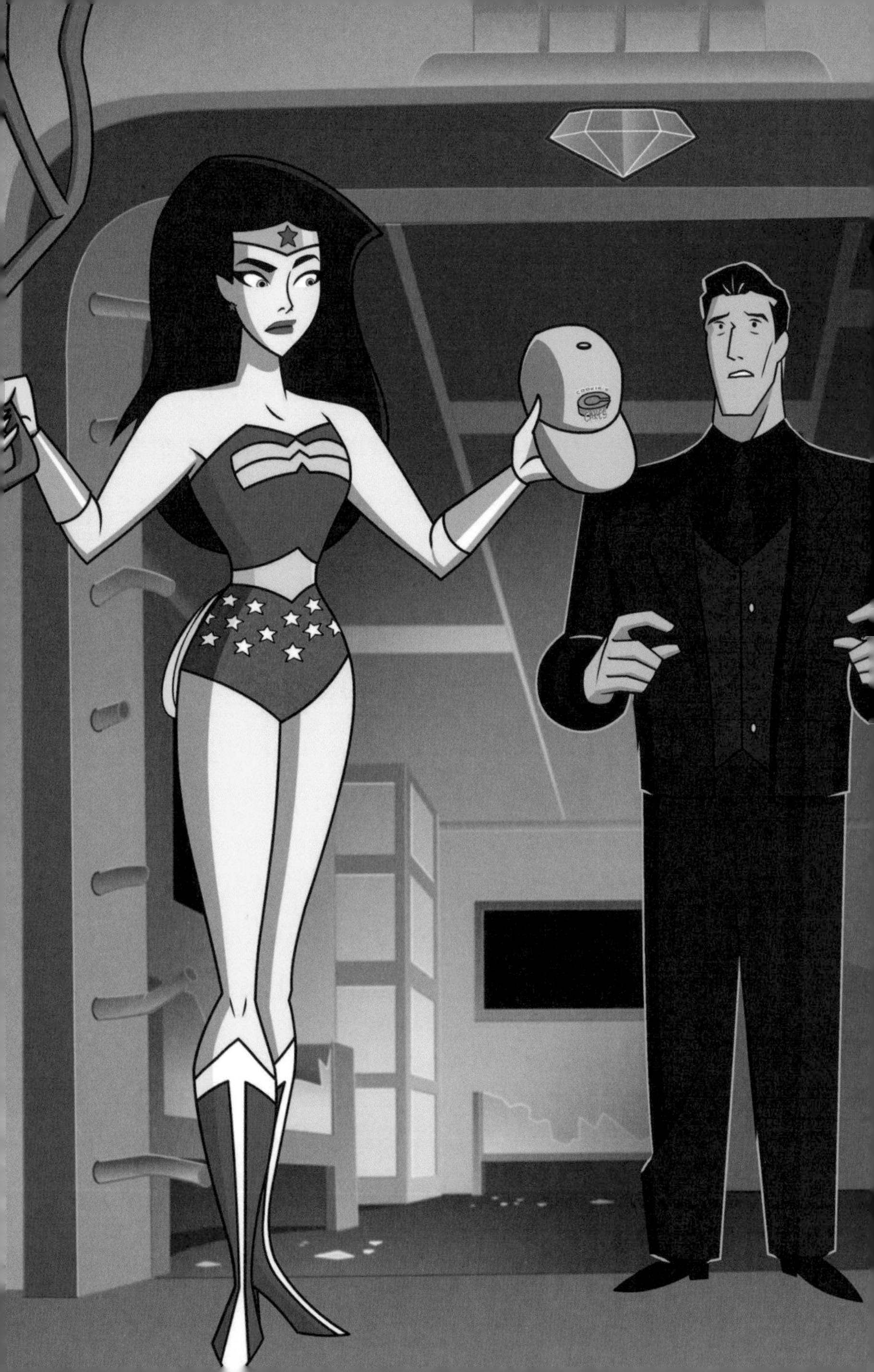
COOKIE'S
CAKES

CRRRREEEAAAK!

With one hand, Wonder Woman reached over and lifted the heavy gate. With her other hand, she pulled the object free. It was a baseball cap. The words "Cookie's Cakes" were written on it.

"What is 'Cookie's Cakes'?" asked Wonder Woman, setting the gate down gently.

"It's a bakery here in the mall," Lieutenant Schorr said.

"It looks very familiar," she muttered.

"All of the employees that work there wear the hats," Schorr said. "It's probably just one of those things you've seen around but never really paid attention to."

"Yes," Wonder Woman said. "That is probably all it is."

CHAPTER 2

CAUGHT IN THE ACT

Three days later, Wonder Woman soared high above the city in her Invisible Jet. Formed from an alien crystal that can take any shape Wonder Woman wills, it was the easiest way to watch over the city.

In the days since the mall robbery, there had been several more mysterious thefts all around the area. The police could not find a single clue at any of the locations.

As her jet passed over the city, Wonder Woman kept her eyes open for anything out of the ordinary.

Ahead of her was the Dodge Building. The sixty-six-floor skyscraper was a famous landmark built in 1930 by newspaper tycoon Walter Dodge. The top floor had been the great publisher's private penthouse. The Dodge family still lived there, along with a fortune in art and expensive jewelry.

Passing by, Wonder Woman glanced at the great stone gargoyles that decorated the balcony around the penthouse. At just that moment, she saw a sight she never could have expected to see 700 feet off the ground — someone was slipping into an open window below the balcony!

With a thought, Wonder Woman ordered the plane to hover above the Dodge Building. Then she leaped from its cockpit.

Sailing through the air like a kite, Wonder Woman pointed herself to the open window. At the last moment, she pulled up and landed gracefully on the narrow ledge beneath it.

Wonder Woman peered around the window. The slender, shadowy figure was dressed all in black. It silently passed through a door just ahead. Wonder Woman pulled herself through the window. Then she hurried across the room and through the door. Down the hall were stairs leading up to the penthouse floor.

Moving with the speed and grace of Diana, the goddess of the hunt for whom she had been named, Wonder Woman raced up the stairs. Suddenly, she found someone else in her path!

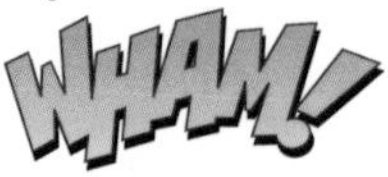
WHAM!

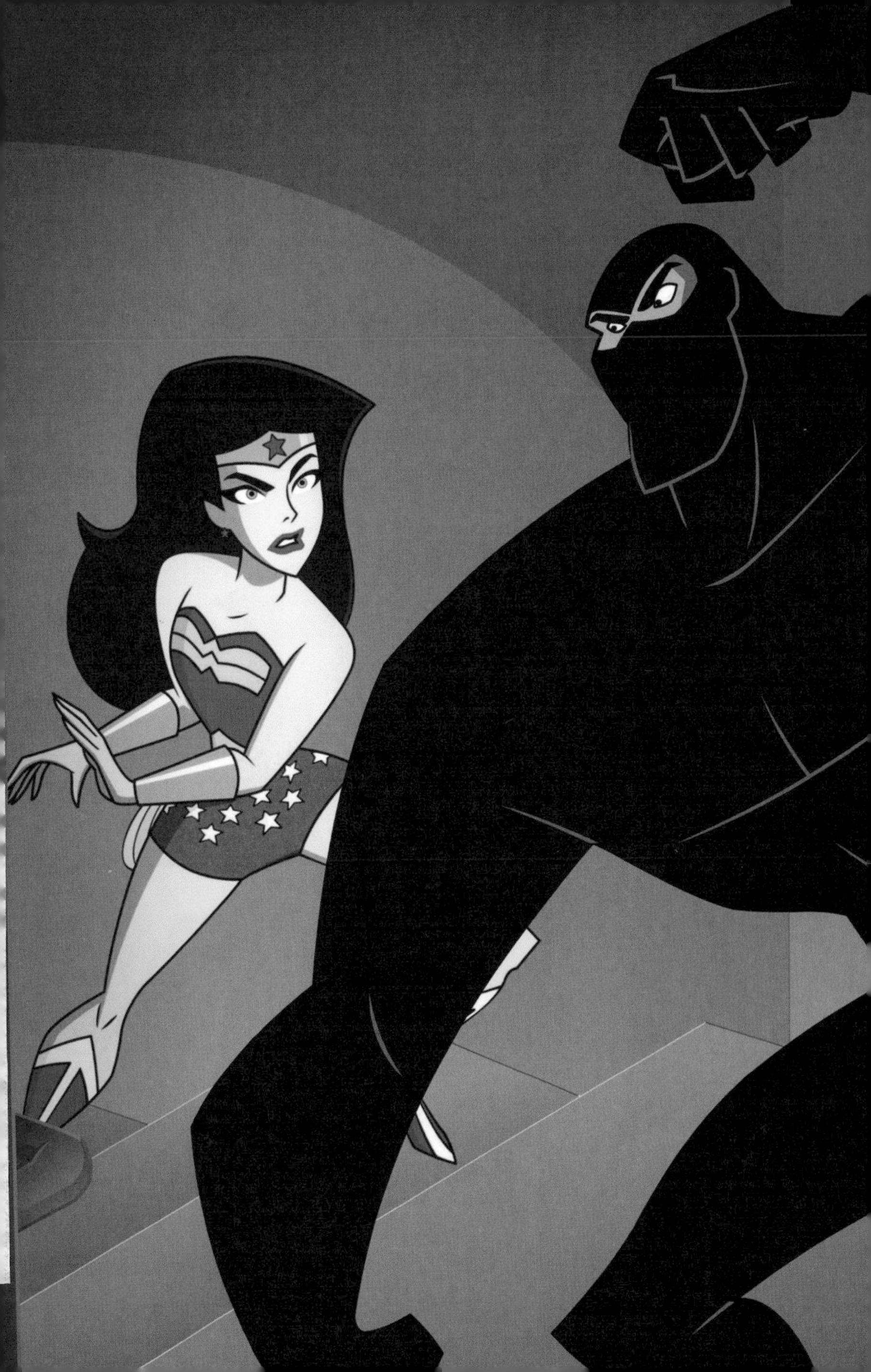

Wonder Woman tried to go around the massive figure, but he threw up a muscled arm and knocked her back. This figure was also dressed in black, but he was almost seven feet tall! His shoulders were wider than most doorways, and his arms and legs were thick with muscle.

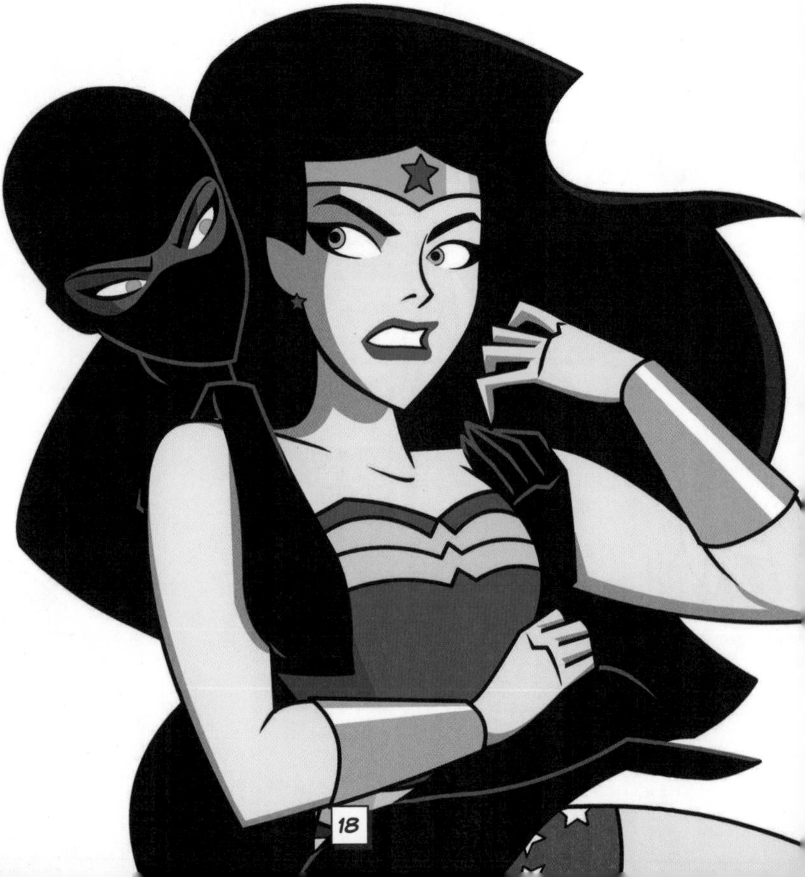

Wonder Woman grabbed her Golden Lasso and swung it at the giant figure. He dodged to one side, and then the thin shadow hurtled out from behind him.

"Now!" the smaller shadow cried.

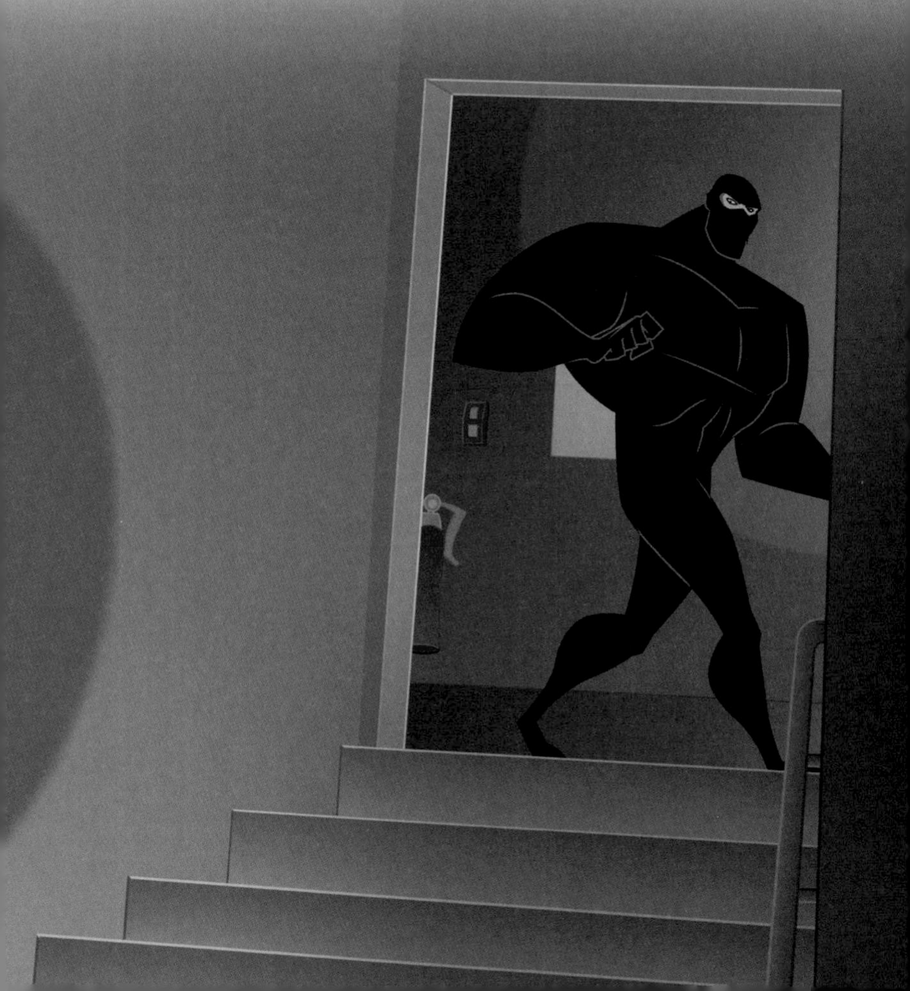

SPPROINGG! The shadowy figure leaped onto Wonder Woman. The Amazon Princess gasped for air as the lean figure wrapped around her like a human snake. It tightened to her arms and legs, too slippery to grasp. How could she fight something that moved as though it had no bones?

Wonder Woman suddenly found herself tumbling down the stairs, her foe slipping from her grip. She tumbled and rolled until she hit the bottom. **SLAM!** As she got back on her feet, she saw the shadow race through the door.

She found her way through the open door and onto the balcony. But by the time she got there, somehow both figures had disappeared — as if by magic!

CHAPTER 3

THE MISSING PERSONS

"What are these crooks, ghosts or something?" Lieutenant Schorr asked.

"They were both very real and solid," Wonder Woman said. "But I'm not sure how they vanished, either."

The Amazon Princess sat down at the lieutenant's desk at the police station. The robbers had stolen a safe filled with priceless jewelry from the Dodge Building. The larger man had ripped the safe from the wall. They took it with them when they fled and then fell off the face of the planet.

"They're not the only ones who've been disappearing," said the policeman. "I have six missing persons cases in the last week."

"Is there anything I can do to help?" Wonder Woman asked.

Schorr pulled a file folder from a stack on his desk and handed it to her. "Probably not," he said. "They are ordinary working people, no problems at home or at work. They all vanished without a trace."

FLAP! FLAP! Wonder Woman flipped through the stack of police reports of the missing people at super-speed. They all came from different parts of the city and worked in many different kinds of jobs.

Suddenly, a familiar face was looking up at her from the folder. "I know this man!" she said in surprise.

"It says his name is Arnold Davis," Wonder Woman added, pointing to the picture of a man with red hair. "I saw him several nights ago at the circus. He bumped into me and was acting strangely. But more importantly, Lieutenant, Mr. Davis was wearing a yellow Cookie's Cakes baseball cap. Just like the one I found at the mall!"

*   *   *

The fairgrounds were once again ablaze with light. The entire place was filled with the laughter of the hundreds who had come to celebrate the Bartleby Brothers Circus' last night in town.

"I still can't believe you spotted one of my missing persons," Lieutenant Schorr said, grabbing a handful of popcorn from a bag.

"But even better, you tied him and the rest of the missing people to the robberies and the circus!" the lieutenant added.

"Well, once we knew Mr. Davis had been to the circus, it was easy for your officers to check if any of the other missing people had visited," Wonder Woman said.

"But I never would have figured out that Arnold Davis worked for the company that monitors the mall's security system," said Lieutenant Schorr. "He must have arranged it so the robbers could get around the cameras and alarms."

He offered Wonder Woman some popcorn. "One of the missing people worked in the office on the floor below the apartment in the Dodge Building," the lieutenant said. "It's possible he could have helped the thieves get inside."

"The others have jobs at or near the other places that were robbed," Schorr continued. "What I still don't get, though, is the connection between that and the Bartleby Brothers Circus."

"That's what we've come to find out," Wonder Woman said. "Let's split up and look around."

The circus was spread out around the main tent. Under the Big Top, clowns, acrobats, and aerialists entertained the crowds with a spectacular show. Around that, smaller tents housed different acts and attractions.

Wonder Woman watched three clowns race across the fairway to the Big Top. Their faces and hair were a rainbow of colors, and they all wore outrageous costumes. One was tall. Another was regular height.

The last clown was a little person with a white face, bald head, and big smile painted on. He seemed nervous and began sweating when he saw Wonder Woman watching him.

Thinking that his reaction was curious, the super hero followed the clowns into the Big Top. As Wonder Woman passed through the entrance, she was surprised at the size of the Big Top tent. It rose far above the height of a three-story building. At the top of the tent hung two trapezes and a long tightrope stretched between two platforms. Atop each platform stood an aerialist, each dressed in fancy, colorful tights.

"Ladies and Gentlemen!" announced a deep on Wonder Woman's left. "Prepare to feast your eyes on our main attraction — the Bartleby Airborne Ballet!"

"Oooohs" and "Ahhhhs" filled the tent. The two aerialists soared through the air, attached to the trapezes by their feet. As they reached the height of their swings, they each released their holds and flew straight toward each other.

WHOOOOSH! They narrowly avoided colliding, and grabbed hold of the other's trapeze after they passed.

They flew back and forth, releasing their swings, tumbling through the air, and gracefully catching on to the moving ropes. The entire crowd was in awe. You could hear a pin drop as the amazing acrobats performed their routine. *This is a very impressive show,* thought Wonder Woman. *And probably a little dangerous.*

As if on cue, a loud noise suddenly echoed through the silence. **SNAP!**

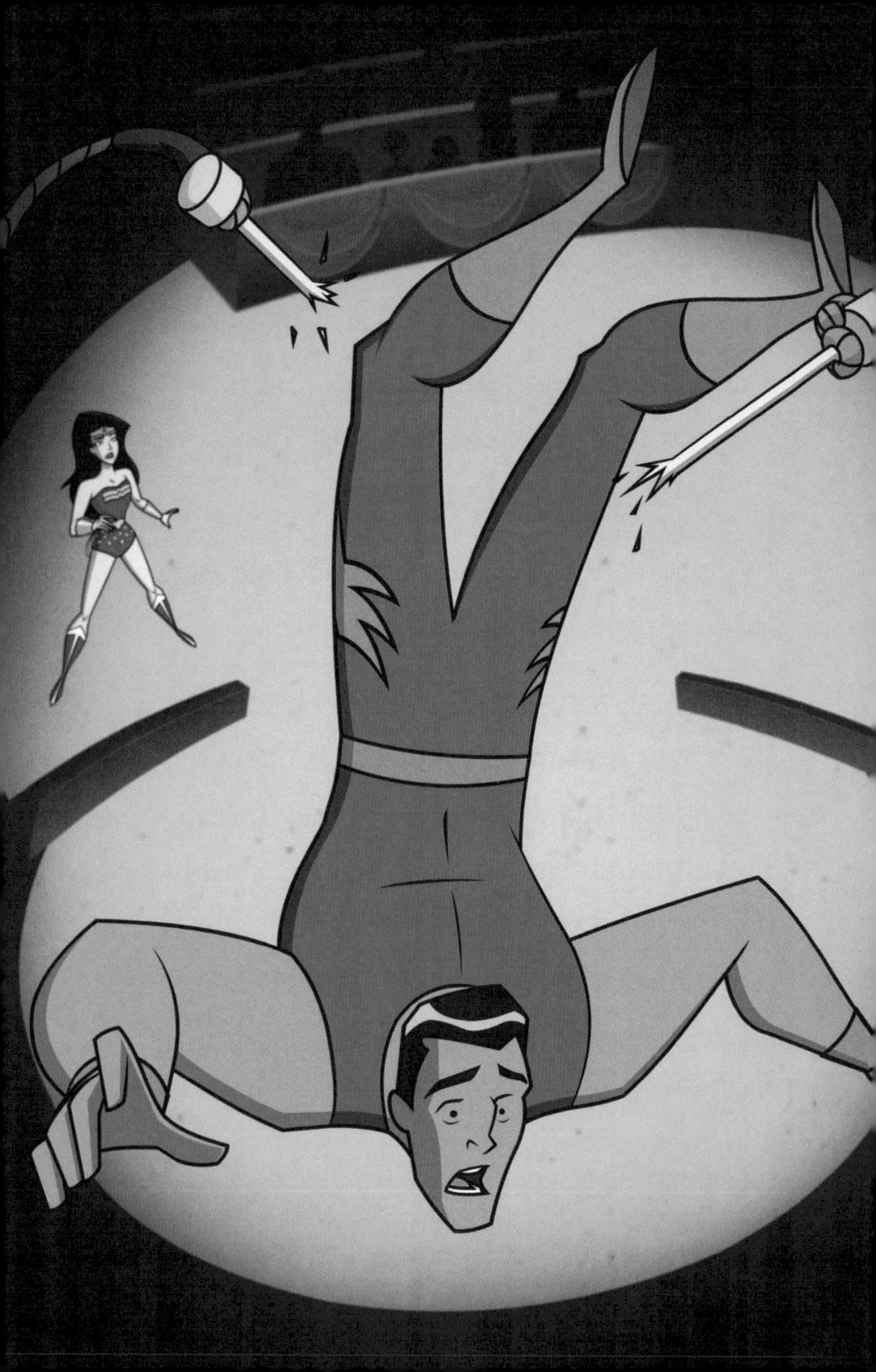

A shrill scream rang out in the tent.
Then someone yelled, "That man's rope just
broke!"

Everyone in the tent immediately gasped
as they saw one of the aerialists begin
to fall. "Someone help him!" cried an
audience member.

Wonder Woman's eyes shot to the
ground and noticed there was no safety net.
*If I don't do something, that man will surely
fall to his death!* thought the super hero.

In a split second, Wonder Woman had
dashed to the center of the Big Top. *FLAP!*
She gently caught the falling aerialist in
her strong arms. For a moment, all was
silent once again. But after a few seconds,
the entire audience burst into cheers!

The applause were nearly deafening inside the Big Top. In fact, everyone in the tent was on their feet, cheering and applauding. Everyone except, Wonder Woman noticed, the strange little clown.

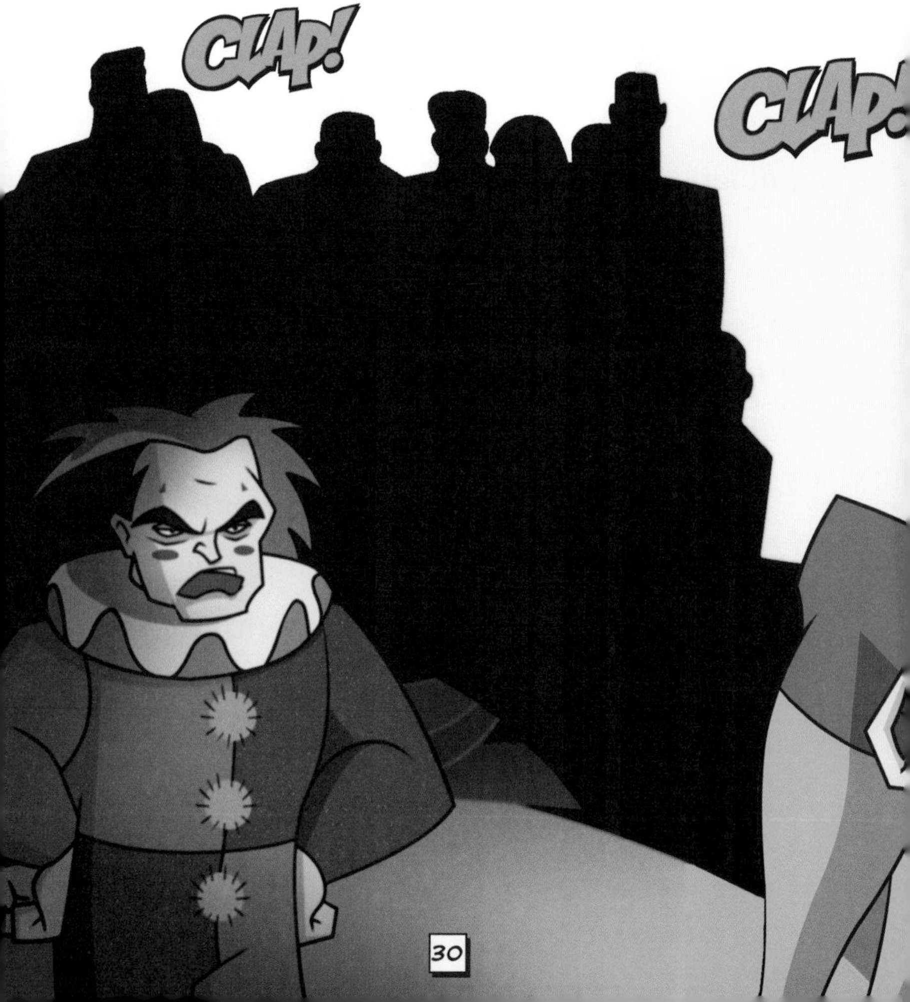
CLAP!
CLAP!

The clown stood nearby, staring at Wonder Woman with an evil look. Then finally he turned and disappeared into the crowd of onlookers.

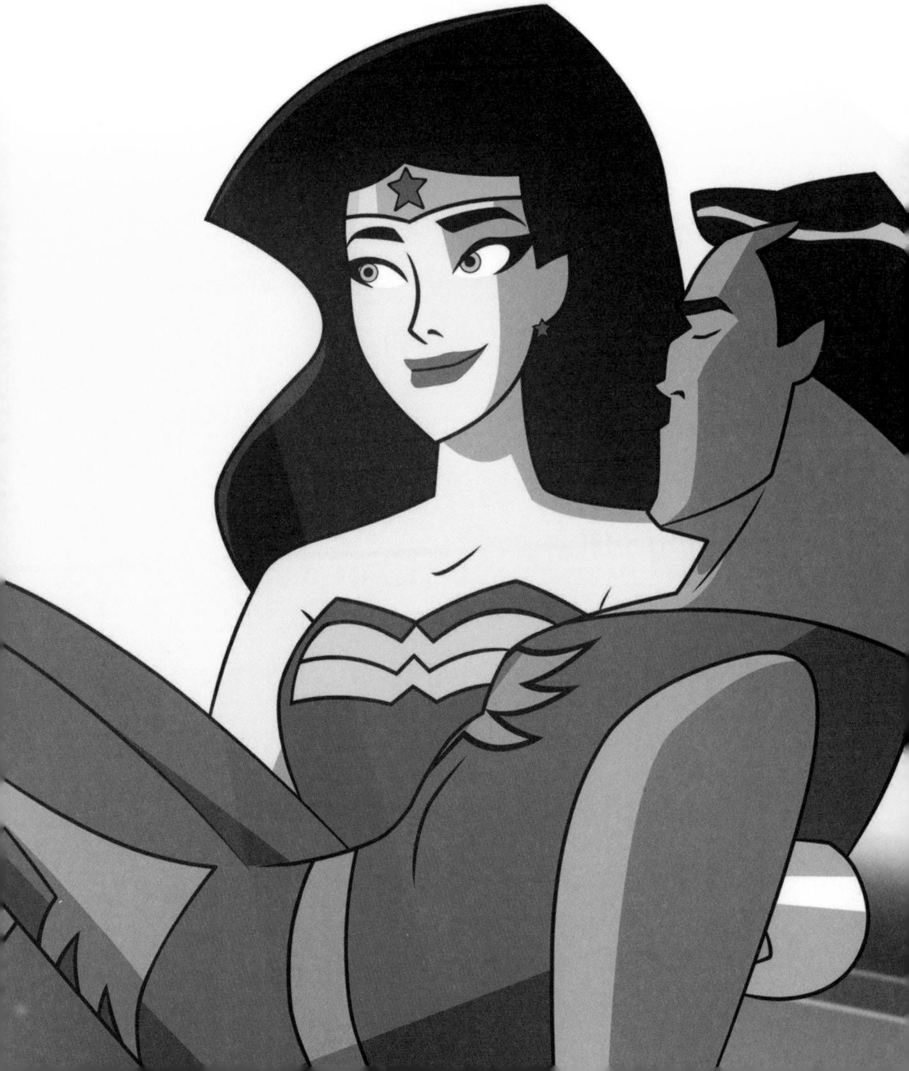

CHAPTER 4

CIRCUS SUSPICION

"How does it feel to be a circus star?" Lieutenant Schorr asked Wonder Woman outside the Big Top tent.

"I'm just glad no one was hurt," Wonder Woman said. "Did your search turn up anything suspicious?"

"Nothing yet," the lieutenant said. "However, we still have to check some of the midway tents."

The midway contained smaller tents that housed special acts and attractions.

Once again, Wonder Woman and Lieutenant Schorr split up to cover ground faster.

Wonder Woman went inside each tent. She saw jugglers juggling balls, knives, and even chain saws. She watched the snake charmer handle deadly creatures like they were harmless pets.

She applauded the skills of the nimble dancers, including a woman who could twist and bend her body like a snake. Her flexibility was truly amazing.

Next, Wonder Woman wandered through the Hall of Mirrors. The maze reflected back twisted images of her beauty.

Then she marveled at the strength of the strong man. He was so big and strong for one who was a mere mortal from Earth.

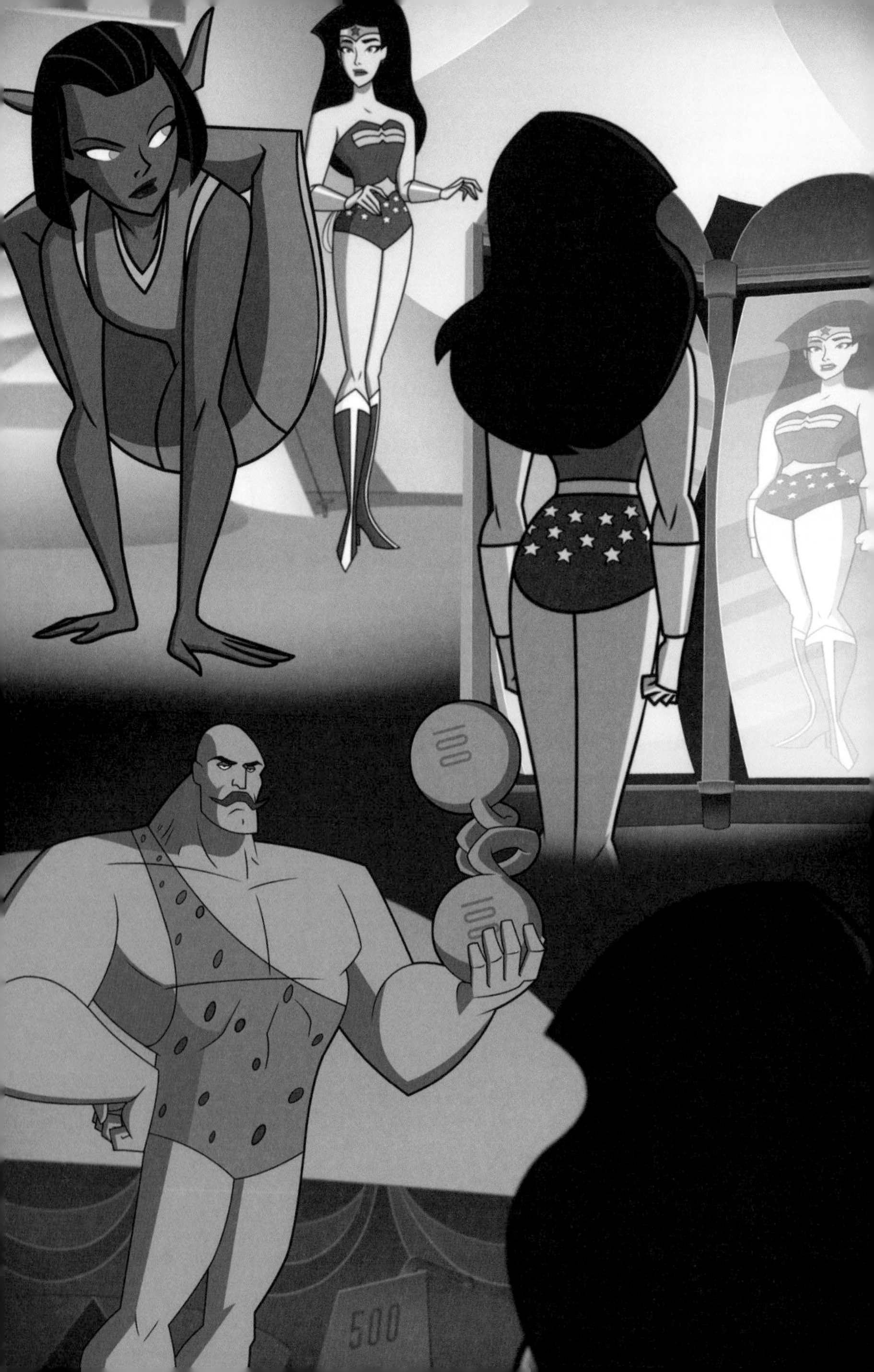
100
100
500

Wonder Woman came across many amazing sights and sounds, but she saw nothing that was out of place for a circus.

She went into the last tent. Like all the others, it held about fifty people who could stand and watch the performer on a small stage. In this tent was Madame Rosa. The sign over the stage said she was a psychic.

When Wonder Woman entered, Madame Rosa, a black-haired woman dressed in a colorful skirt, had a young man from the audience on stage with her. She had hypnotized him and was asking him silly questions about his life and work. His truthful answers made everyone else in the tent laugh.

Except, noticed the Amazon Princess, for Madame Rosa's assistant — the strange clown Wonder Woman had seen before.

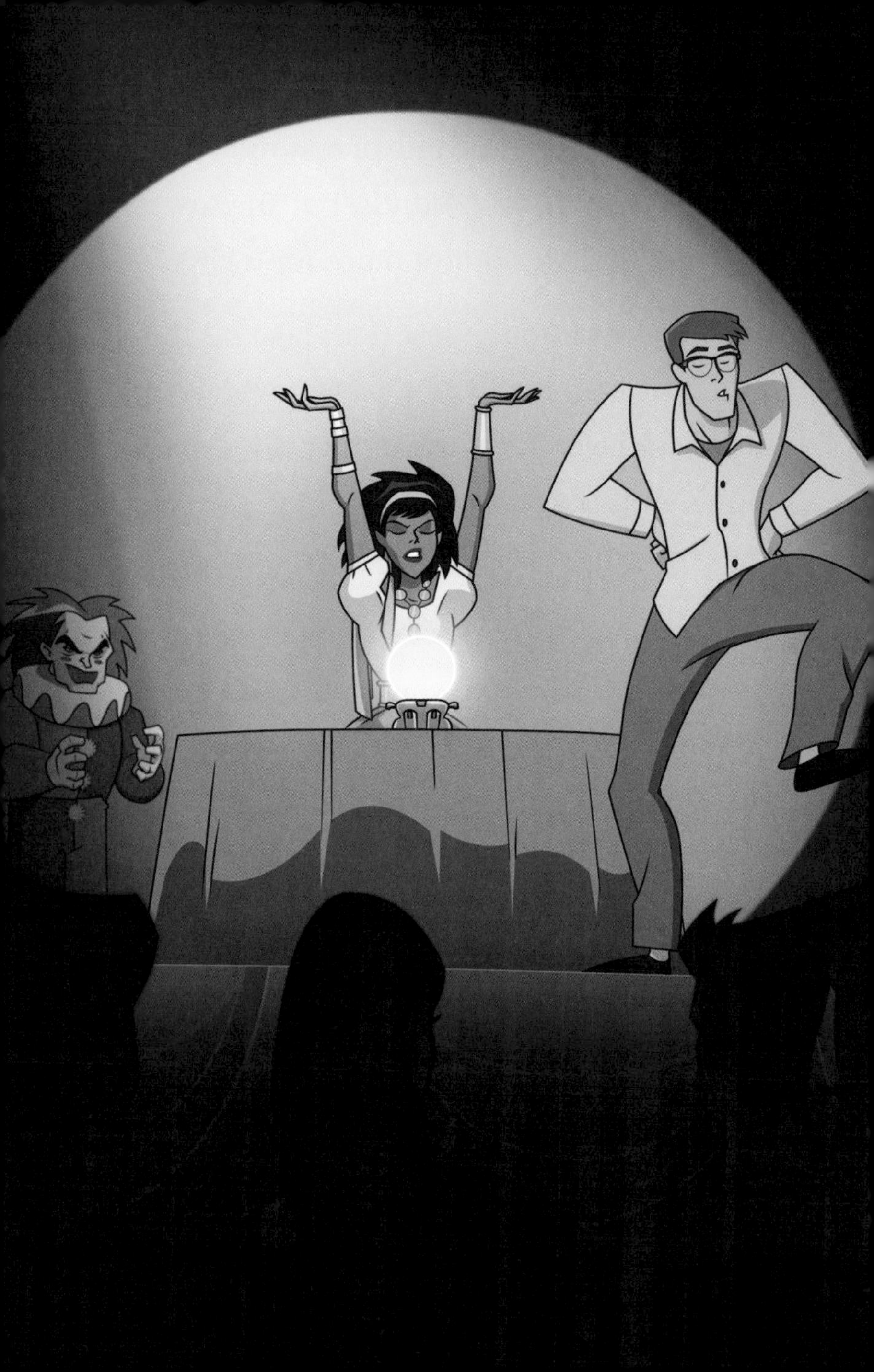

Under the makeup, the little man gestured at Madame Rosa with his hands and glared with his dark, menacing eyes.

Madame Rosa turned back to the hypnotized man and snapped her fingers. This released the man from his hypnotic trance. **HAHAHAHA! HAHAHAHA!** The crowd laughed at the man. He smiled shyly, but looked confused as he returned to his friends. With that, the show was over.

Wonder Woman and Lieutenant Schorr met by the Big Top. "Looks like this was a waste of time," said the policeman.

Out of the corner of her eye, the super hero saw the little clown. He was peeking out from the entrance to the Big Top, watching the princess and the police officer.

"I'm not so sure about that," she said.

Wonder Woman turned to look at the lieutenant. "That little clown over there has been acting strangely all week," she said.

"Maybe it's just a coincidence," said Lieutenant Schorr with a shrug.

"Maybe, maybe not," she said. "But I think I'll go ask him a few questions."

When Wonder Woman turned back toward the little clown, he was gone. "That's odd," she said. "He disappeared."

"Well, that *was* the last show of the night," said Lieutenant Schorr. "He must have gone home. We should probably leave, too, Wonder Woman."

The super hero nodded, and said, "Yes, I suppose I *should* head home for the night." But Wonder Woman knew she would be up for some time to come.

CHAPTER 5

UNDER THE BIG TOP

One hour later, the fairgrounds were empty and dark. In the still of the night, the circus was a quiet, lonely place.

Only one, eerie light was still shining in the Big Top. Inside, several of the circus performers stood in the center ring. They were silent and standing at rigid attention.

Their eyes stared straight ahead, looking at nothing. They did not even look at the little man in the colorful clown costume as he paced back and forth in front of them.

"I was not pleased to see Wonder Woman today," said the clown. His voice was deep, yet strangely soothing. "Why was she here?"

The strongman, the tall thin woman whose body twisted and turned like a snake, and Madame Rosa did not answer. Neither did the aerialists who stood nearby. They were all like statues, unmoving.

"It is good that today was our last in this city," the clown said. "In the morning, we will move on to a new city for more looting."

"I believe those plans have changed, Doctor," said a woman's voice from the darkness.

The clown gasped. "Wonder Woman! Quickly — capture her!" he ordered.

At the sound of his command, the circus people suddenly sprang into action.

CLICK! A searchlight blazed on, tracing a finger of light through the darkness. Wonder Woman was highlighted high above on the aerialist platform.

"I'm right here!" Wonder Woman said.

The little clown pointed and screamed out, "Get her!"

The acrobats started to climb the rope ladder up to the pedestal board. Wonder Woman waited until they were halfway up. Then she grinned and stepped off of the platform. She sailed down and landed softly in front of the clown.

"I see you're up to your old tricks, Doctor Psycho," Wonder Woman said. "Still trying to brainwash everyone?"

"Not everyone," Doctor Psycho said. He laughed, and added, "Just the ones who won't do what I say!"

Wonder Woman had met Doctor Psycho before. He used his psychic powers and super-hypnotic abilities to control people and make them commit crimes.

Suddenly, a pair of thick, muscular arms wrapped around Wonder Woman from behind. They began to squeeze her tightly.

"I see," said Wonder Woman. "You must be the strongman who ripped the security gates off at the mall stores."

The Amazon flexed her arms and flung the strongman off her like an insect. He crashed into the seats. WHAAAMMMMM!

But before she could reach for Doctor Psycho, the snake-lady coiled around her.

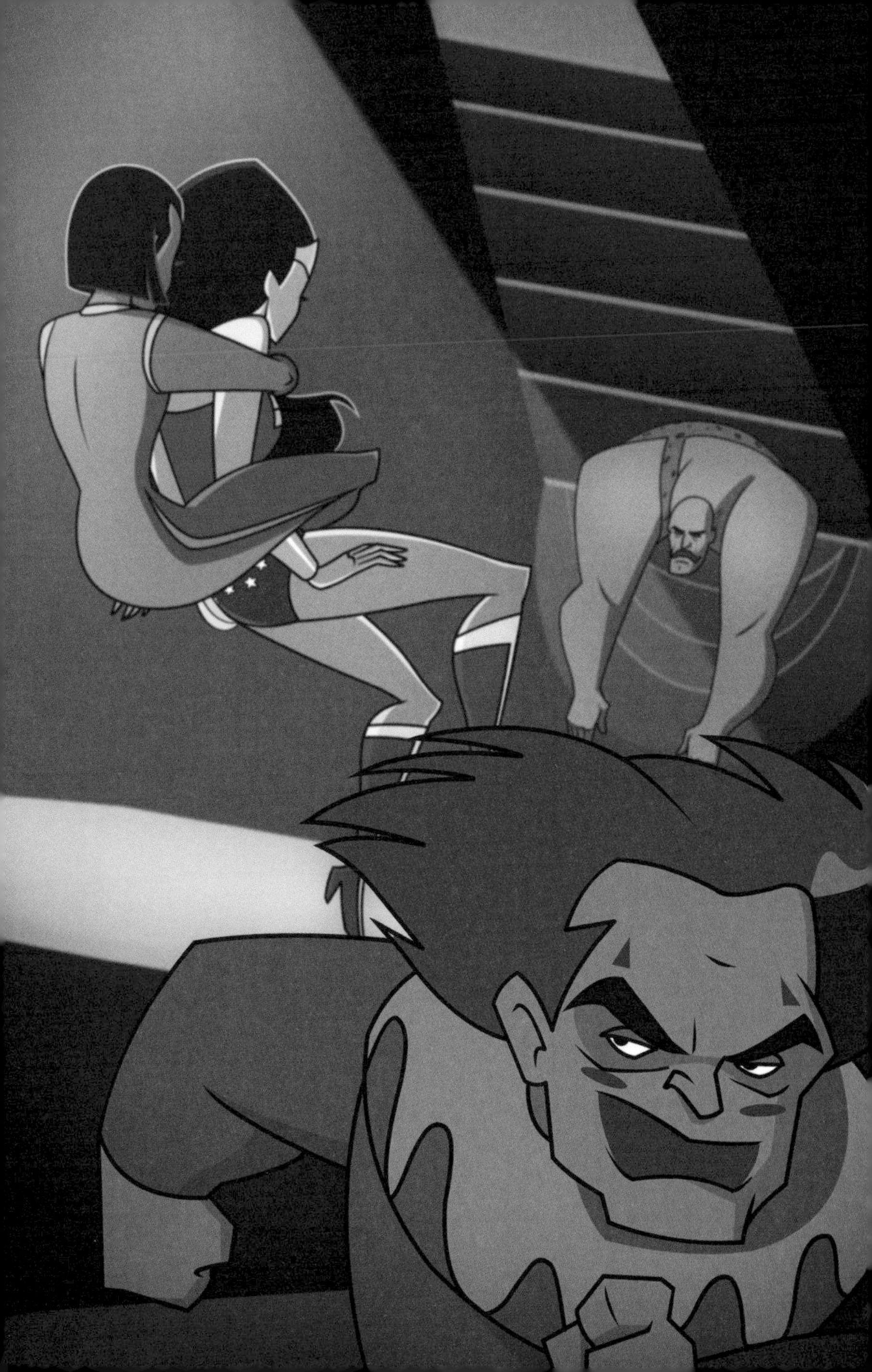

Wonder Woman fell forward and hit the ground. **THUD!** Unhurt, she looked back at the face of the hypnotized contortionist wrapped around her midsection.

"And you must be the contortionist who climbed up the side of the Dodge Building," she said, smirking.

"Very clever," said Doctor Psycho. He turned toward the tent entrance and started running. "I hypnotized them all to be my servants! Just as I hypnotized the people Madame Rosa found in the audience to help commit crimes near where they worked or lived."

Wonder Woman rapidly twisted, sending the hypnotized woman to the ground. Suddenly, all three acrobats came jumping, leaping, and tumbling right at her.

Wonder Woman sidestepped the first tumbler and threw him to the ground with a **THUD!**

As the second leaper dived at her, she ducked, rolled to her back, and kicked him over her. He went flying and crashed into a pole. **CRUNCH!**

Wonder Woman caught the third one by the ankle. She spun in a circle three times and then released him. **CRASH!** He collided with the first acrobat, who had just been getting back to his feet. They landed together in a heap. **WHAM!**

When Wonder Woman had finished with Doctor Psycho's henchmen, she turned her attention to the criminal mastermind. However, he had already left the Big Top tent.

Wonder Woman dashed outside at super-speed. As she exited the Big Top tent, she heard the sound of police sirens echoing through the night air.

Just then, Wonder Woman caught a brief glimpse of the clown impostor. He was running into the Hall of Mirrors sideshow tent across from the Big Top tent. She wasted no time and quickly followed him inside.

"You can't get away, Doctor," half a dozen Wonder Women called out, all different sizes and shapes in the mirrors. "You might as well make this easy on yourself and surrender now. There's nowhere for you to hide."

"Upon reflection," Doctor Psycho shrieked, "I think this is a great hiding place."

Doctor Psycho stepped into view, right in front of Wonder Woman. His grin ran the entire width of his face. "Come and get me," the crazy clown challenged.

Wonder Woman dived right at him, but she simply shattered a mirror. SMAASSHHH!

As Wonder Woman returned to her feet, Doctor Psycho appeared again — but this time, he had eleven reflections!

Doctor Psycho's laughter echoed around her. HAHAHAHA! HAHAHAHA!

"You'll never figure out which one is the real me!" he said.

"Maybe I don't need to," she said.

Wonder Woman ran back outside. With a single mighty tug, she pulled the entire tent to the ground! WHOOOOSH!

 The sound of mirrors smashing filled the air, followed by Doctor Psycho's shrieks of anger.

Wonder Woman and Lieutenant Schorr pulled Doctor Psycho out from under the tent. He was dazed and no longer a threat.

"Nice work, Wonder Woman," said Lieutenant Schorr. "I'll bet he never expected you to pull the whole tent down!"

"He should have, lieutenant," Wonder Woman said with a smile. "Because unlike him, I never clown around."

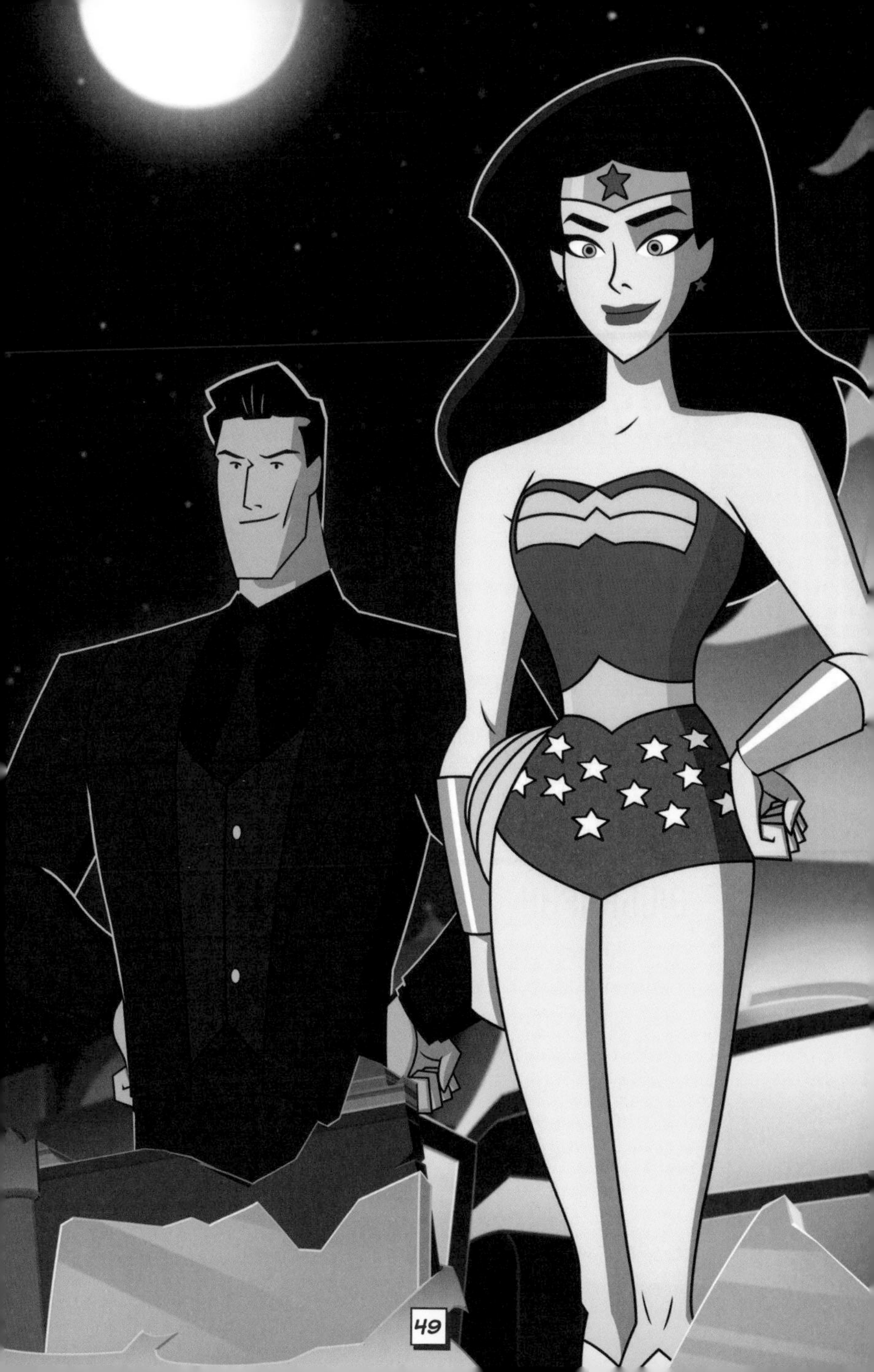

INVISIBLE PLANE
SECRET FILES

FILE NO. 3765 >>>DOCTOR PSYCHO

ENEMY ›› ALLY FRIEND

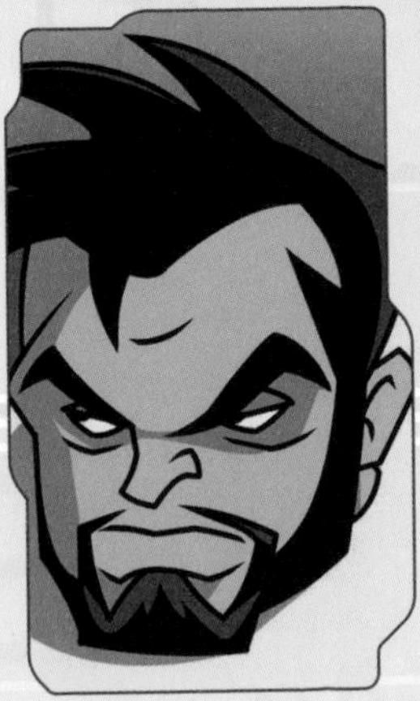

REAL NAME: Edgar Cizko

OCCUPATION: Psychotherapist

HEIGHT: 3' 9" **WEIGHT:** 85 lbs

EYES: Blue **HAIR:** Black

POWERS/ABILITIES: Able to attack people's dreams; can create real-life nightmares to frighten victims; hallucinogenic powers; telepathy.

BIOGRAPHY

Although his appearance can be deceiving, Dr. Psycho is one of Wonder Woman's deadliest enemies. This evil madman murdered Dr. Charles Stanton, a respected psychiatrist, and stole his identity. Then he attempted to use Stanton's likeness to control Wonder Woman with his mental powers. Although his plan failed, Dr. Psycho hasn't given up his quest to "cure" the Amazon Princess of her sanity.

NO FEAR

Doctor Psycho's strength lies in his ability to read people's minds and use their worst fears against them. In order to effectively combat this master telepath, Wonder Woman will have to steel her resolve and make her will as strong as her armored bracelets. She must face her own worst fears before the evil Doctor can use them against her. The only way to fight fear is to make oneself fearless — something the Amazon Princess excels at. Her Lasso of Truth will also be quite handy, since honesty overcomes fear.

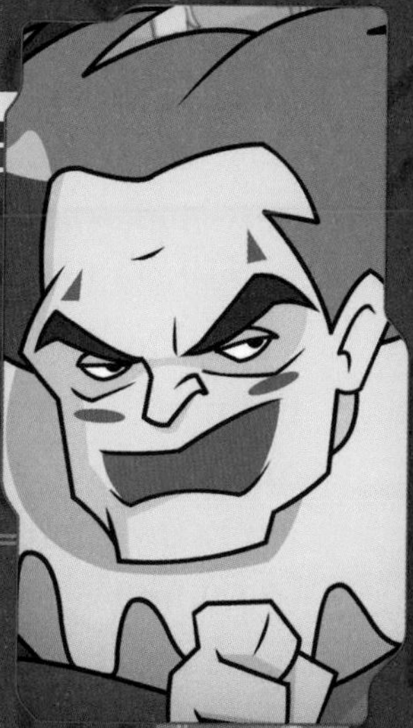

KNOW YOUR ENEMY

WHO IS DOCTOR PSYCHO?

Telepathy (tuh-LEH-puh-thee) — communication of one person to another by thoughts alone

Psychotherapist (sy-koh-THER-uh-pist) — a doctor who treats psychological problems

Hallucinogenic (huh-loo-suh-nuh-JEN-ik) — causing hallucinations

Hallucination (huh-loo-suh-NAY-shuhn) — if you have a hallucination, you experience something that does not actually exist

BIOGRAPHIES

Paul Kupperberg has written many books for kids, like *Wishbone: The Sirian Conspiracy*, *Powerpuff Girls: Buttercup's Terrible Temper Tantrums*, and *Hey, Sophie!* Paul has also written over 600 comic book stories starring Superman, the Justice League, Batman, Wonder Woman, The Simpsons, Archie and Jughead, Scooby Doo, and many, many others Paul's own character creations include Arion: Lord of Atlantis, Checkmate, and Takion. He has also been an editor for DC Comics, Weekly World News, and World Wrestling Entertainment.

Dan Schoening was born in Victoria, B.C. Canada. From an early age, Dan has had a passion for animation and comic books. Currently, Dan does freelance work in the animation and game industry, and spends a lot of time with his lovely little daughter, Paige.

GLOSSARY

aerialist (AIR-ee-uhl-ist)—a person that performs feats above the ground, often on a trapeze

ambassador (am-BASS-uh-dur)—the top person sent by a government to represent it in another country

contortionist (kuhn-TOR-shuh-nist)—an acrobat able to twist the body into unusual postures

hypnotize (HIP-nuh-tize)—to put someone into a trance

looting (LOOT-ing)—the act of stealing from a store or house, usually during a riot

mythology (mi-THOL-uh-jee)—a collection of myths, or stories about gods and goddesses

psychic (SYE-kik)—a person able to tell what others are thinking or predict the future

psycho (SYE-koh)—a mentally unbalanced person

trapeze (tra-PEEZ)—a horizontal bar hanging from two ropes, used by circus performers

DISCUSSION QUESTIONS

1. Some people are afraid of circus clowns. What kinds of things are you afraid of?

2. Doctor Psycho uses fear to control others. Can fear ever be a good thing? Why or why not?

3. This book has ten illustrations. Which one is your favorite? Why?

WRITING PROMPTS

1. Have you ever been to a circus? If so, what was it like? If not, what sorts of shows would you want to experience? Write about circuses.

2. Wonder Woman has to solve a mystery in order to defeat Doctor Psycho. Have you ever figured out something that someone didn't want you to know? What happened? Write about your puzzle-solving experience.

3. Design your own circus. What will you name your circus? What kinds of sideshows and main events will it have? Write about it.

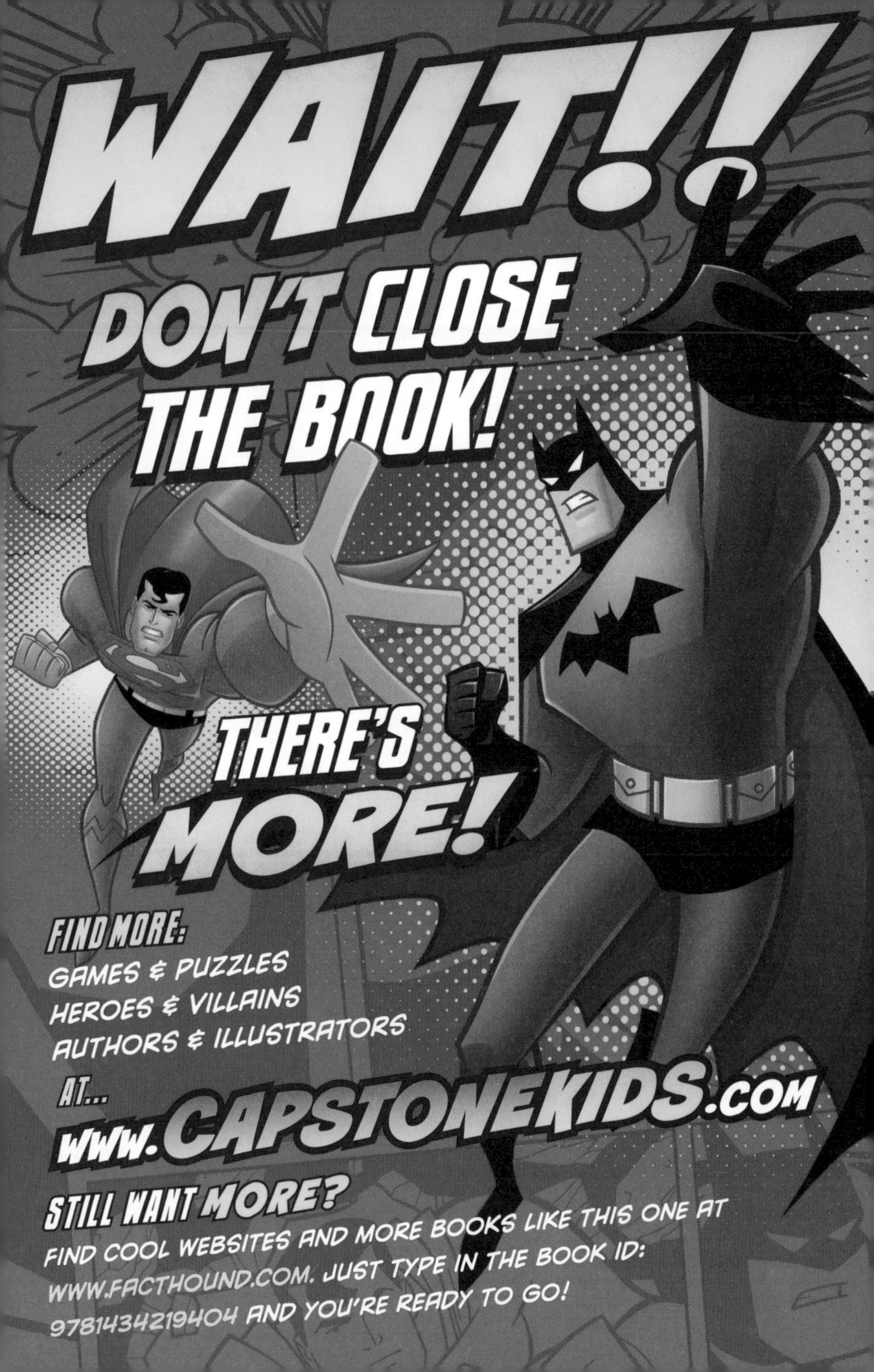
WAIT!!
DON'T CLOSE THE BOOK!
THERE'S MORE!
FIND MORE:
GAMES & PUZZLES
HEROES & VILLAINS
AUTHORS & ILLUSTRATORS
AT...
WWW.CAPSTONEKIDS.COM
STILL WANT MORE?
FIND COOL WEBSITES AND MORE BOOKS LIKE THIS ONE AT
WWW.FACTHOUND.COM. JUST TYPE IN THE BOOK ID:
9781434219404 AND YOU'RE READY TO GO!

MORE NEW WONDER WOMAN™ ADVENTURES!

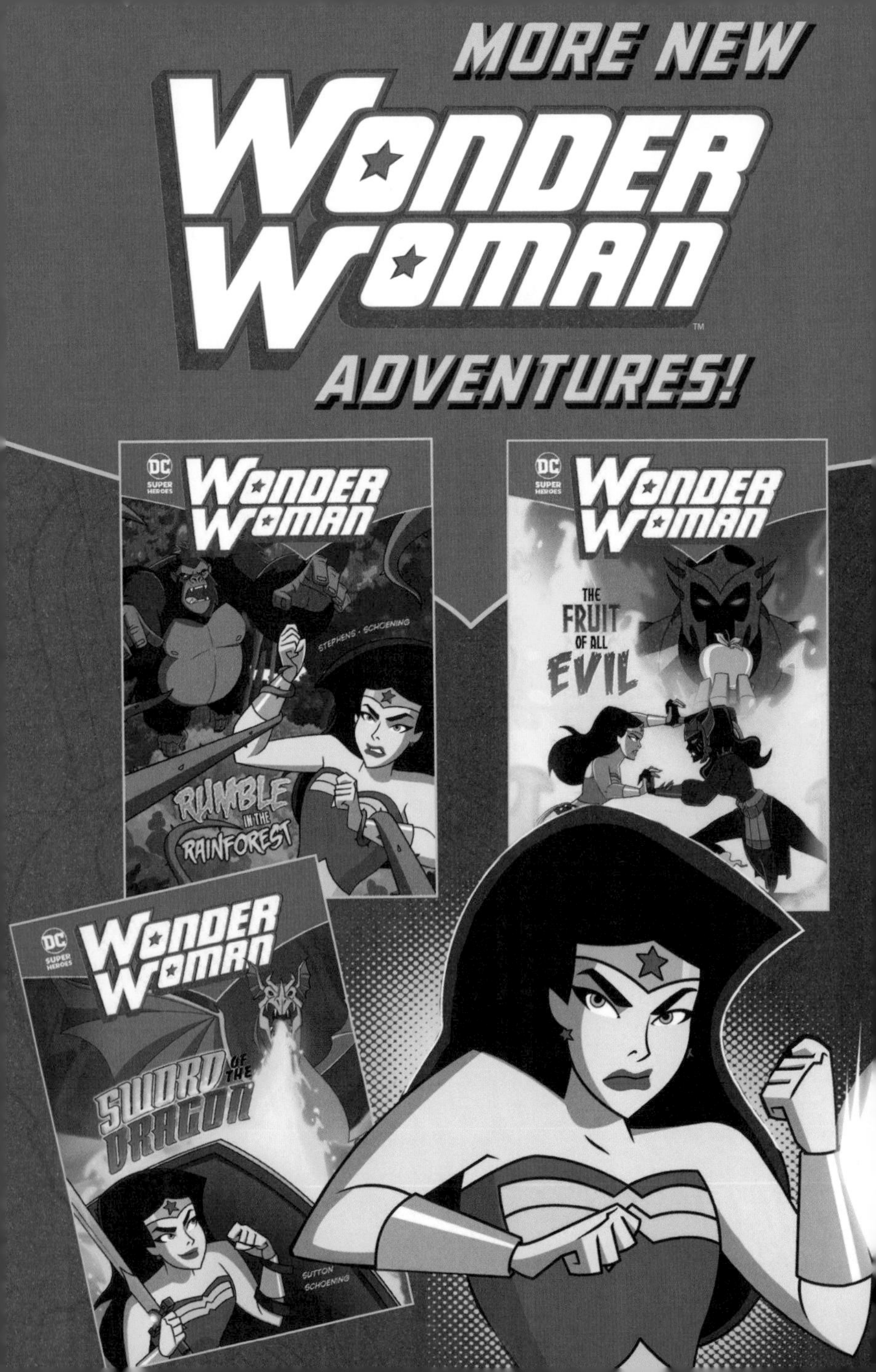
DC SUPER HEROES
WONDER WOMAN
STEPHENS · SCHOENING
RUMBLE IN THE RAINFOREST
DC SUPER HEROES
WONDER WOMAN
THE FRUIT OF ALL EVIL
DC SUPER HEROES
WONDER WOMAN
SWORD OF THE DRAGON
SUTTON
SCHOENING

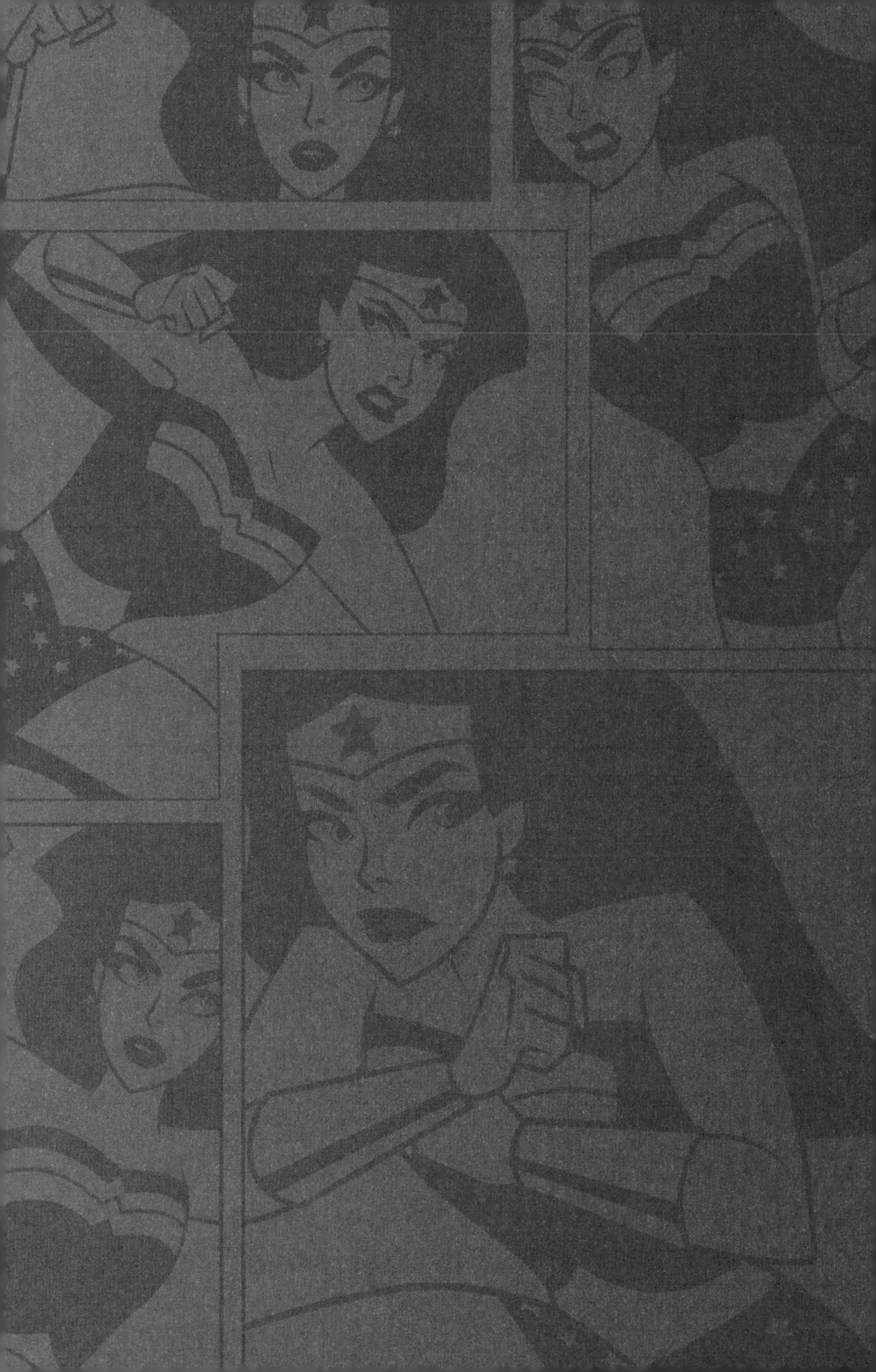

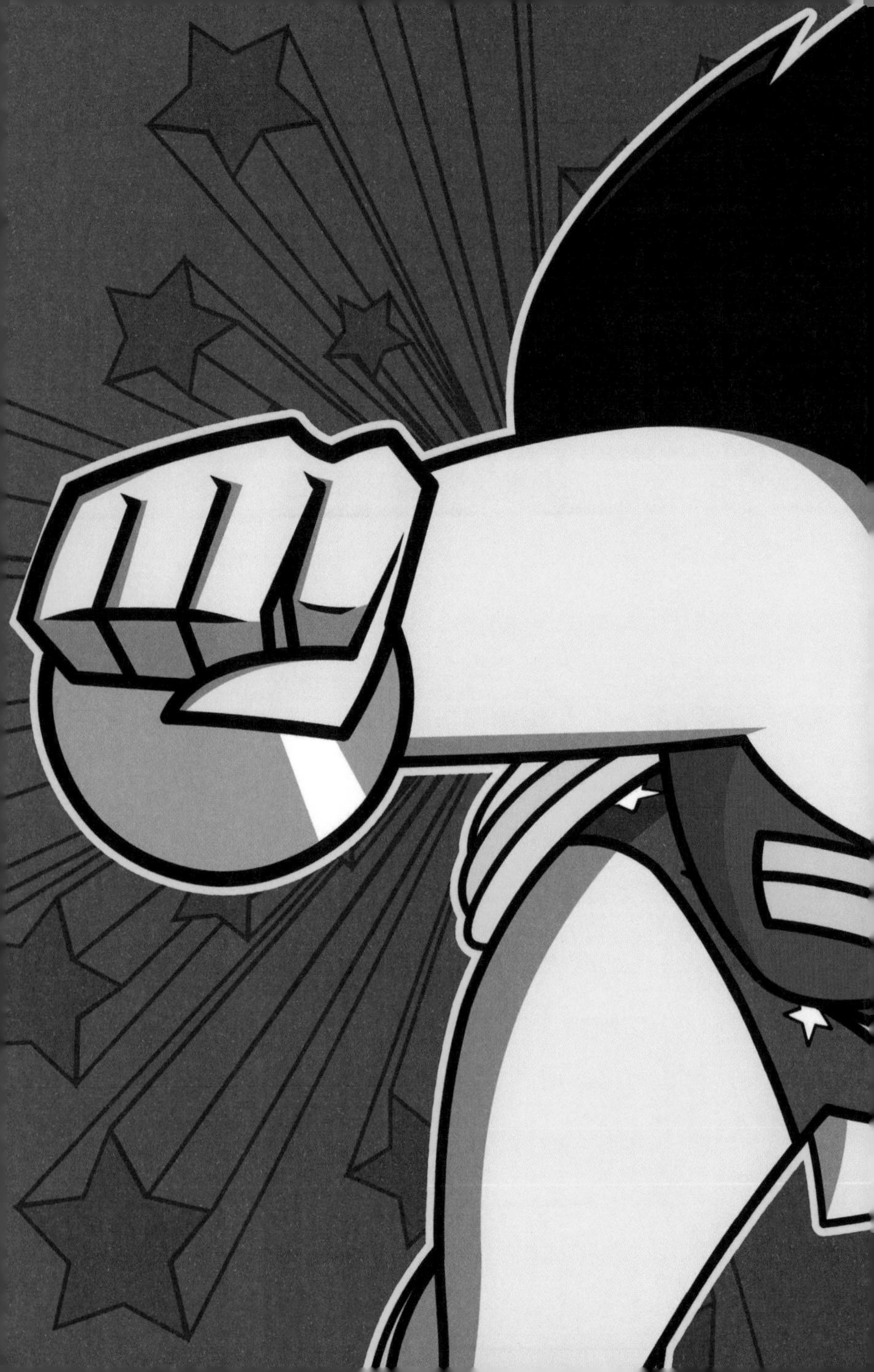

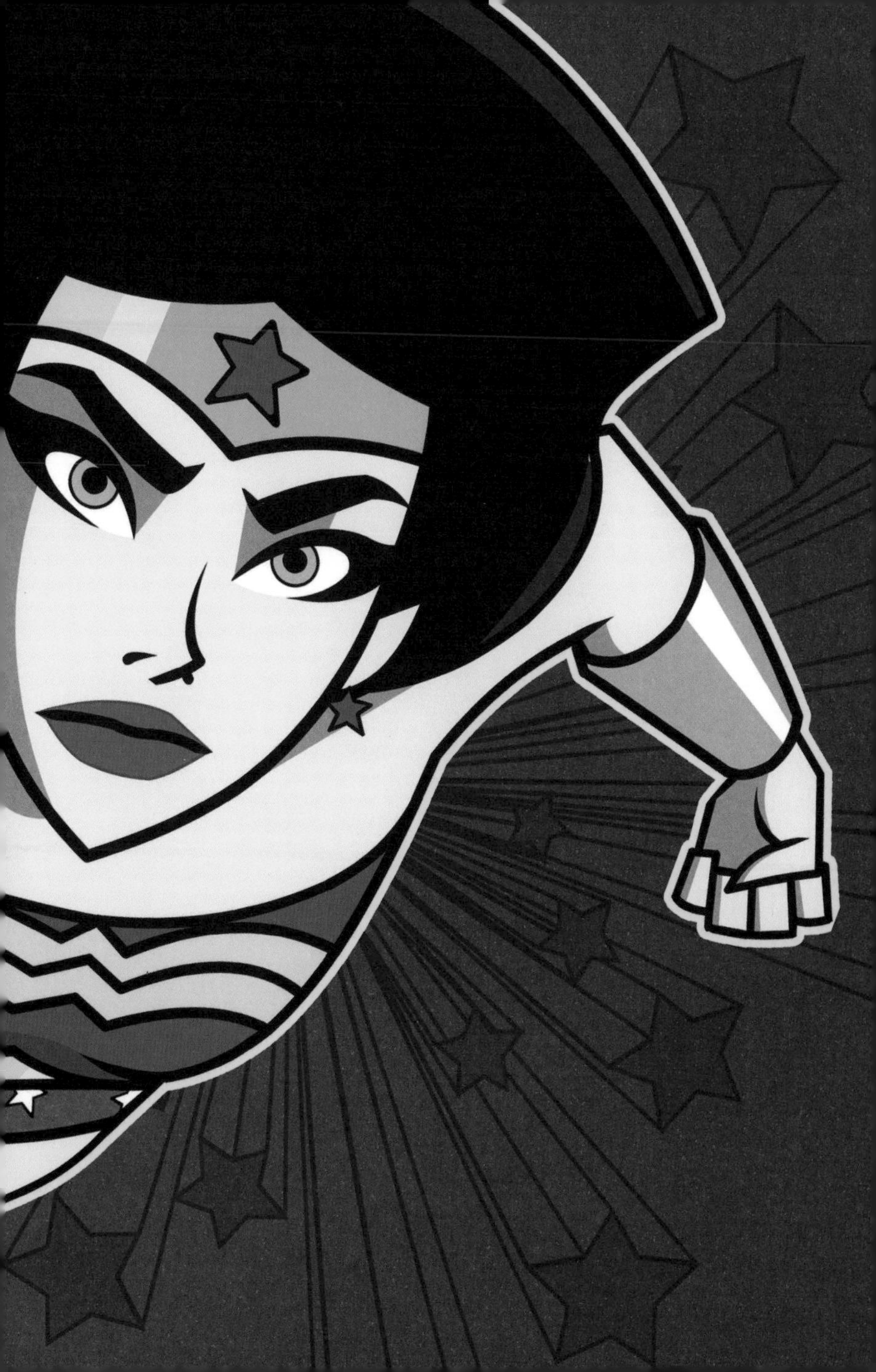